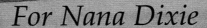

For Nana Dixie

First published in Great Britain 1995
by Andersen Press Ltd.
First U.S. edition 1996
First Voyager Books edition 1999
*Voyager Books* is a registered trademark of
Harcourt Brace & Company.

LC 95-30754
ISBN 0-15-200834-9
ISBN 0-15-202110-8 pb
Printed and bound in Italy by Grafiche AZ, Verona
A C E F D B

# BOO!

## Words and pictures by
## *Colin McNaughton*

VOYAGER BOOKS
HARCOURT BRACE & COMPANY
*San Diego    New York    London*

Through the dark, dark streets of the dark, dark town, Preston the Masked Avenger sneaks....

"Boo!" says Preston the Masked Avenger, and he disappears into the night.

Slinking through the shadows,
Preston the Masked Avenger
spies Billy the Bully,
his next victim....

"Boo!" says Preston the Masked Avenger, and he disappears into the night.

Catlike, Preston the Masked Avenger slides through the darkness until he reaches the schoolhouse, where his teacher is working late....

"Boo!" says Preston the Masked Avenger, and he disappears into the night.

Next, the superhero
comes to Mr. Wolf's house.
"Boo!" says Preston the Masked
Avenger very quietly as
he sneaks right past.
"I may be a superhero," says
Preston, "but I'm not dumb!"
And he disappears
into the night.

MR. WOLF

NO
WOOD
CUTTERS

Preston the Masked Avenger
lies in wait for the greatest
villain in the universe—his dad.

"Boo!" says Preston the Masked Avenger, and he disappears into the night.

At least, he would have
disappeared if his dad
hadn't grabbed him first.

"Preston!" shouts his dad.
"I've had complaints about you
from all over town. You're
a naughty little pig."

Preston the Unmasked Avenger is sent to his room without any supper.

# Suddenly!

"Boo!" says Preston's dad. "That'll teach you to go around scaring people."

But it doesn't.

# Praise for Preston Pig

### Boo!
"Will be asked for again and again."—*School Library Journal*

### Oops!
"Preston Pig . . . returns with his lupine sidekick to delight audiences once again."—*School Library Journal*

### Preston's Goal!
"An ideal picture book for soccer enthusiasts."—*Kirkus Reviews*

### Suddenly!
"Deftly executed and designed to amuse a young audience."—*Booklist*